HOW NOT TO INVADE EARTH

Art and Writing by
Russell Nohelty

Letters and book design by
Cammry Lapka

Proofreader
Katrina Roets

Published by Wannabe Press
Paperback ISBN: 978-1-942350-60-6

Special thanKs:

Jason Bowen, Walter Weiss, Salvator Tierno Sr, Paul Nygard, Andrea Johnson, Myrddin Starfari, Cat BanKs, Larry Gilman, Daniel Groves, Steven Brunwasser, Philip R. Burns, Lisa Lyons, Michael H Bullington, Peter the Astronomer, Victoria Nohelty, and ChucK Robinson.

This is such a weird booK, and I am so amazingly blessed to have people in my life that believed in it enough to give it a a chance. This booK was sitting on my hard drive for five years and only exists out in the world because of you.

Hi, Trap.
Hi, Reck.
Watcha doin?
Nothing.
Just gonna blow up the Moon.
You're what?!
Gonna blow up the Moon.

Hah.
Funny joke.
uh huh.

That is a joke, right?
Ummmm...

No.
PUSH!

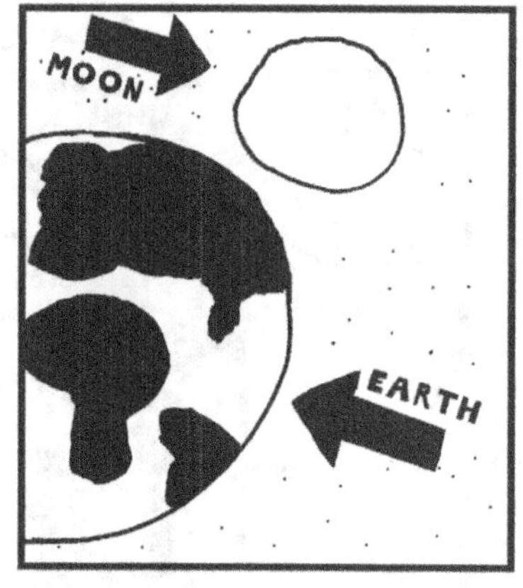

MOON
EARTH

'SPLODER

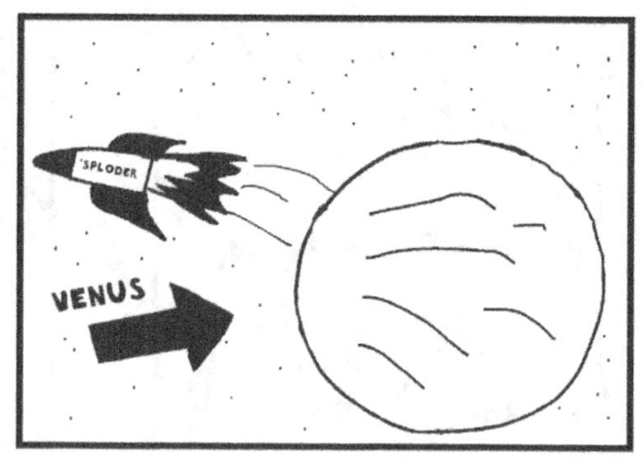

'SPLODER
VENUS

SPLODE!!
OH MY!
OH YEAH!
OH NO!

Gotta get home!
Mom! Dad!
Shut yer up, you!
Yeah. Quiet yer you.
You don't understand. The Moon just 'sploded!
You and your crazy imagination.
It's not— just look outside!
Nah.
Now, go to your room.
You're grounded.
Aw man.

I can't believe what you did!
We're gonna get in so much trouble.
You think?
That could be fun.
Hey!
What's the big idea?
That's it.
I'm outta here.
I am not taking the fall for this.
Prepare to be retaliated against!!!
I wouldn't do that.
Shut up, you!

ATTACK!

TAP
TAP
TAP

DEFENSIVE LASER BLAST!

SPLODE!

Those were my best ships.

You 'sploded them.
Told ya.

Hi, Sis.
Why do you look so glum?
Moon 'sploded, but no one believes me.
I believe you.
You do?!
Of course, dum dum. I got eyes, don't I?
Then I'm not crazy.
I didn't say that.
Come on. We gotta find shelter.
Isn't this house shelter?
No.
Oh. Okay, I guess.

Hello, this is the President of Earth.
I understand you are the person, er alien, who blew up our Moon.
What are your demands to stop 'sploding us?
Demands?

Oh, I have a few.

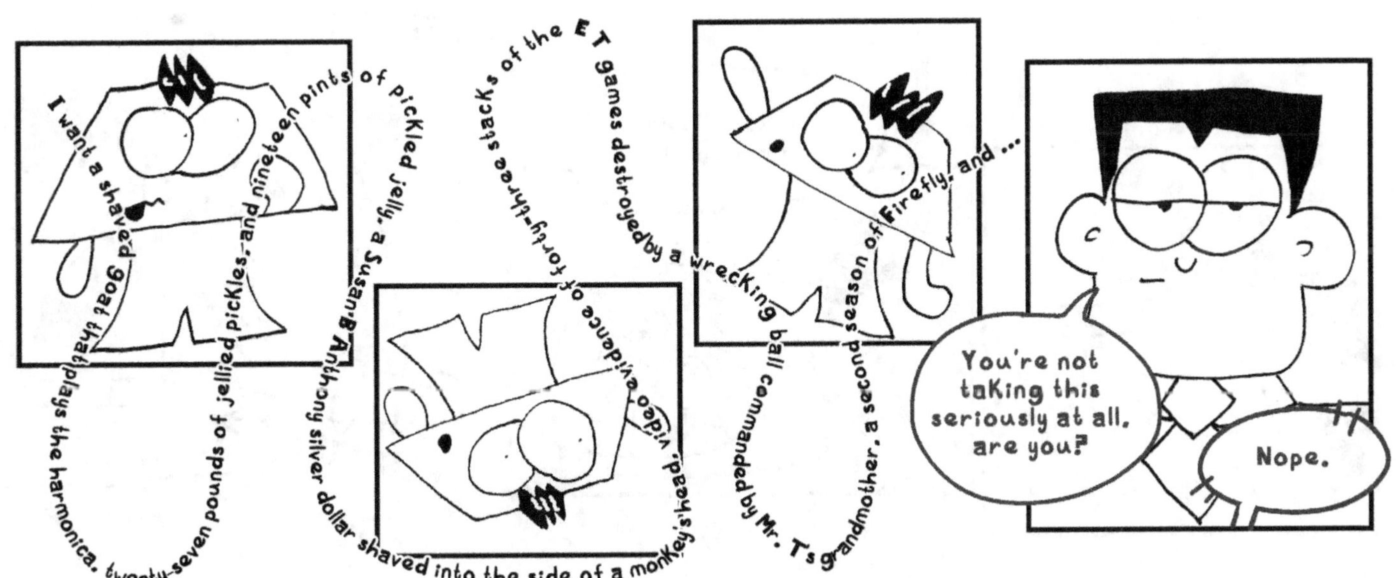

I want a shaved goat that plays the harmonica, twenty-seven pounds of jellied pickles, and nineteen pints of pickled jelly, a Susan B. Anthony silver dollar shaved into the side of a monkey's head, video evidence of forty-three stacks of the ET games destroyed by a wrecking ball commanded by Mr. T's grandmother, a second season of Firefly, and ...
You're not taking this seriously at all, are you?
Nope.

Gotta get out of here.
General! I think they are attacking.
FIRE!
Then fire on them with limited prejudice!

Stupid Trap with his stupid—
Ahhh! 'SPLODER!!!

SPLODE!
EVASIVE MANEUVERS!

Got 'em, sir.

Excellent.

Not good.

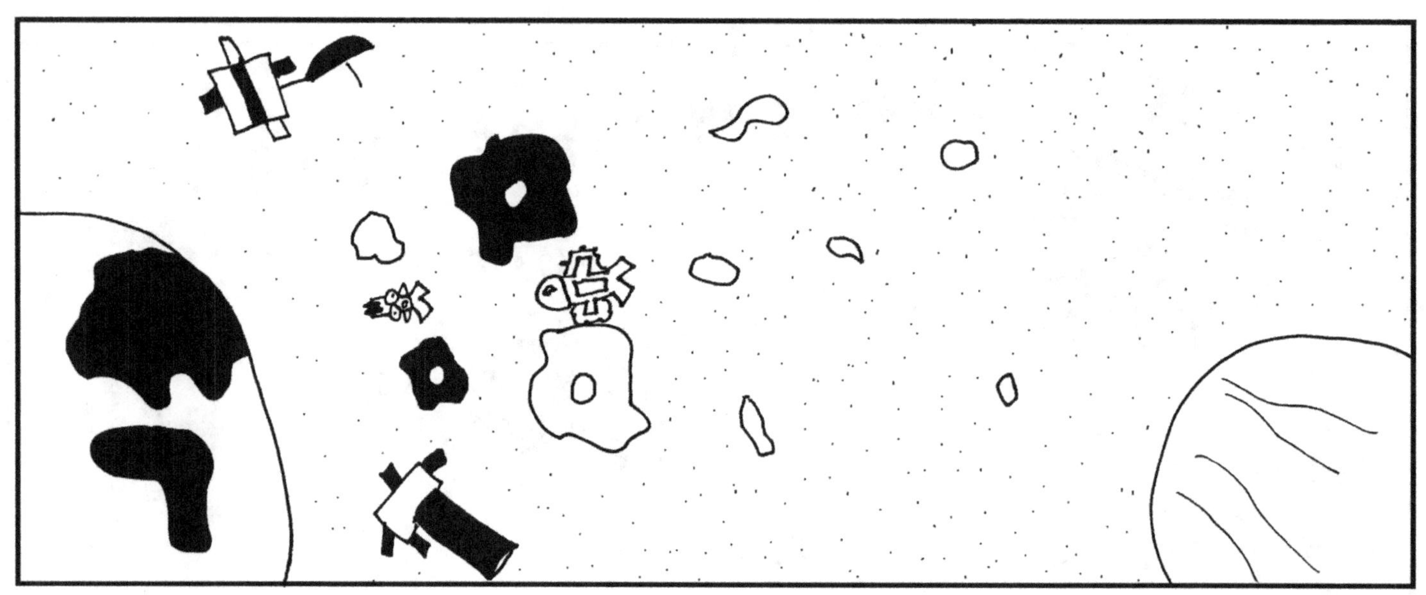

Gotta.
Get.
In.
Spacesuit.
And now to crash into Earth.
This will hurt.

Come on. We can hide in the barn.
How is that better?
BOOM!
We've shot down your advance team.
Advance team?
You mean Reck?
How dare you?
TRAPZODIUS!!!

I see you have requisitioned a thermal detonator.
Yes, boss lady?
You don't have authorization for that.
What game are you playing at?

WEEEEEEEEEEEEEEEEELLLLLLLLLLLLLLLLLLLL
I guess I just really wanted to blow up the Moon.

That is unsanctioned and unauthorized.
Oh. Well. I Kinda already did it.

It's true. We hated it.
Wonderful.
Sorry.

Not only did he blow up the Moon...

...But he sent an attack ship, which we had no choice but to shoot down.

You what?

Please tell me this is a big joke.
Well then.
I hate to tell you this.
'Fraid not, ma'am.
But Earth is in for a whole heap of bad times.
Um, hello?
Are you dead?
No.

Do you
need help?

Yes.
I Know
what to do!

Stay
here!
ZIP!

That ship had RecK on it.
Do you Know what this means, Private Trap?
Well, do you?
Ummmmm...
No.
Do I get soup?
No soup!
It means Venus has to invade Earth and retrieve RecK before he's experimented on.
Oh.
That's too bad about the soup.
War too, I guess.

General Eyeball?
Yes, ma'am.
How is war times prep coming?
We're locked and loaded, ma'am.
Ready to deploy.
What are your orders?
Let's go to war.

Where did you go?
To get some rope.
I'm gonna throw it down to you now.
Okay.

There you go.

Got it.

Pull!

uuuuh!

Grrrrrunt.

YOINK!

CRASH!
Ow.

Corporal Reck!
Corporal Reck, can you hear me?
Stop being a glorm jam and talk to me!
Are you dead?
It's as I feared, Mr. President.
The Martians are going to attack with all they have.
Maybe we should surrender.
I would rather DIE than surrender.

We can't show weakness. What would our enemies think?
It would save millions of people.
Maybe.
But then we would look like wimps. I would rather everybody die than have one person call me a wuss.
Get offa me!
Stupid suit.
So, you're an alien?
Are you here to assimilate us?
Or probe our butts?

We don't really do that.
Is that what humans think about us?
You're here to kill us then, right?
I mean, blowing up the Moon kind of did that, though, didn't it?
Can't live for long without tides.
I didn't blow up your Moon.
Gentlemen, you have trained for this.
And now we are at war!
With an extraterrestrial enemy!
Let's get them.
They're the bad ones!

They ARE the bad ones.
Definitely not us!
We're the good guys.
And we'll 'splode every last one of them to prove it.
I need to get a message to my people before they do something stupid.
Like blowing up the Moon?
That was just one idiot.
Not strong enough.
I mean, I have a short wave radio.
What about the military base?
They have a huge radio transmitter.
I'm not taking a militant alien to a military base!
He's probably a spy.

I'm not militant or a spy.
I'm a pacifist.
See, he's a pacifist.
That's exactly what a spy would say!

Oh no. It might be too late.
We have to hurry before everything 'splodes.

This is
the Blue One.

Approaching targets.

There they are.

I'm in
weapons
range.
Do I have
permission to
engage, captain?
Permission
granted.

Alright.

Let's.
Do.
THIS!

The humans are powering up their weapons.
Do we kill them now or later?

Why not both?

We have to win.

To preserve our way of life.

We must destroy the enemy ships.

Rabble rabble rabble WAR!!
Rabble rabble rabble DESTROY!!

PEW!
PEW!
PEW!
PEW!
PEW!
PEW!
The whole squadron is launching.
We don't have much time. Help me over this fence.
bzzzz
I think it's electrified.

What makes you think that?

Bzzzzzz
SUPER ELECTRIFIED FENCE.
This huge sign that says SUPER ELECTRIFIED FENCE.

I'll bet it's not even on.

See?

FZZZZ ZZTT!

BOOOOSH!

Not good.
Please don't be dead.
I'm going to get in so much trouble.
This is so messed up.
Why are we the ones dealing with this crazy thing?
Ow.
Rabble rabble fight win rabble rabble.
Um, is that a command?
Yeah, what are you saying?
WAR.

What have I done?
I messed up so bad.
This is not fun.

We're losing our fighters!
Man down.
This sucks.
We can't take much more of this.
What are your orders?
This is going so badly.
Half our fleet has 'sploded.

There's too many of them!

Who ordered this stupid mission?!

Oh no. I have a bogie on my six.

And now, 'splosion.

PEW PEW PEW.

KABOOM!!!

GRRRR

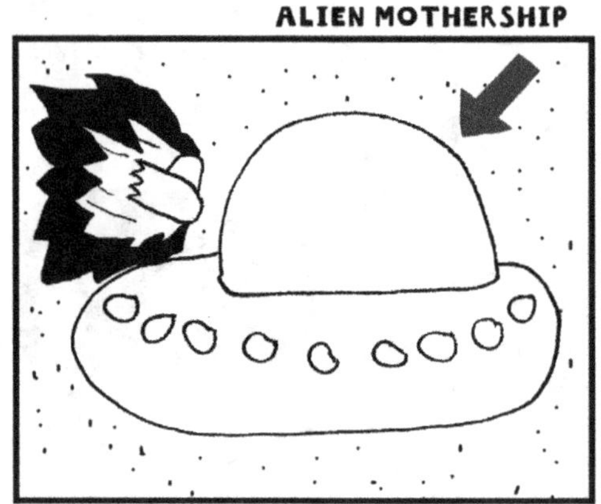
ALIEN MOTHERSHIP

BOOM!

Um, we're pretty well boned out there, General.
I know, private.

I know.

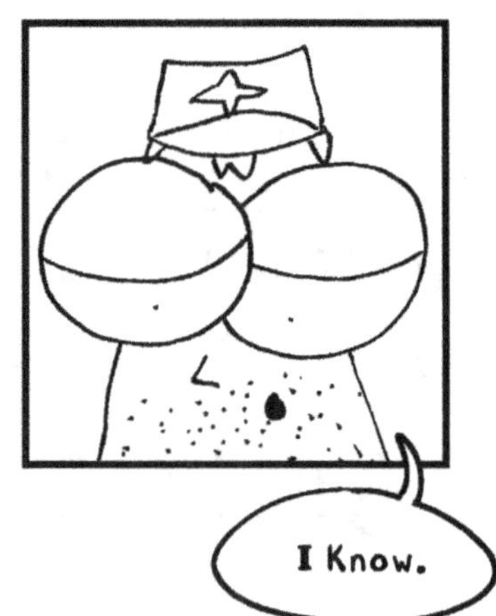
I know.

Let's not do that again.
We have to find another way into the base.
What way? This is a base. It's not a mall. There are not a lot of options.
Maybe we should try the front door.
Oh yeah, the front door.
That's a terrible idea!
Do you see those guards?
Rabble rabble rabble.

I mean, I guess there is one way to get through them.
How?
You're not going to like it.
Try me.
Okay.

DECEPTION!

This is a big hole.
Yup. Somebody should fix it.
Maybe it should be us.
Nah.

uuuuh.

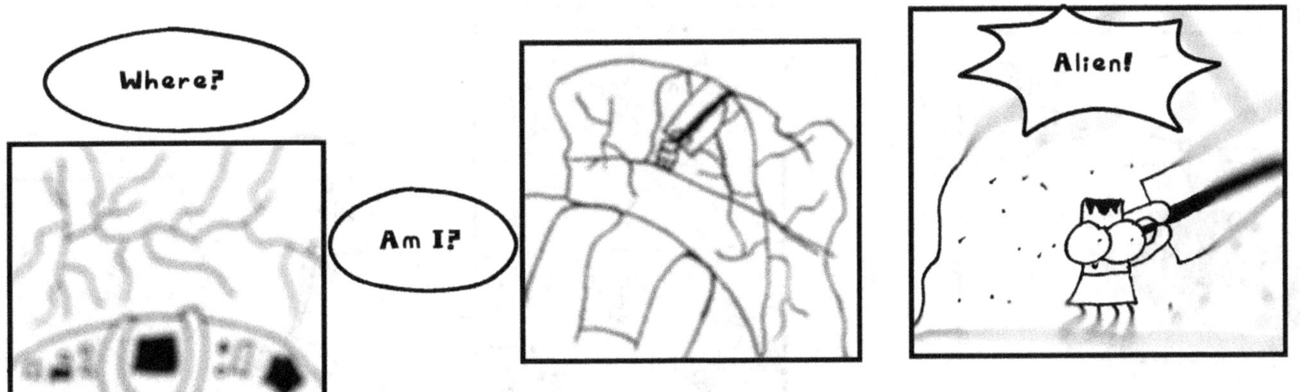

Where?
Am I?
Alien!

EJECT!
POP!

What the—?

Is that?

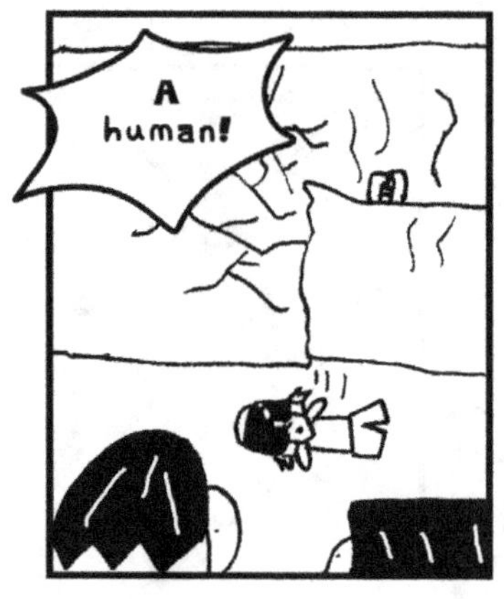
A human!

I better call this in!
Before it eats us!

Uhhhh.

What are you doing?

Bringing you to the base as our hostage.

Hostage?
No thank you!

Let me go!

Hey! Do you want to get into that base or not?
Yes.

Then trust us.

I mean you're only Kids.
So I shouldn't.
But okay, I guess.
Thanks for the vote of confidence, jerK.
Just be cool and maybe this will work.
Love the confidence.
I'm twleve.

Halt!
Stop right there!
You can't hide from us!
That's what you thinK.
YOINK.

Who are you?
Umm.
CLICK.
I'm a lamp.

Alien!
Put your hands up!
Calm down, alright. I'm not the enemy.

I don't believe you.
I mean, I did blow up your Moon.
That's fair.
But I feel really bad about it.

We're losing!
I told you we should have surrendered!
I'm sorry, Mister President, but maybe you're right.
I'll call the aliens and discuss peace terms.
General! There's something you have to see!
This better be good.

So you blew up the Moon?
Yup.
And you sent us to war?
I guess so.
And why shouldn't I kill you?
Cuz I'm real sorry about it?

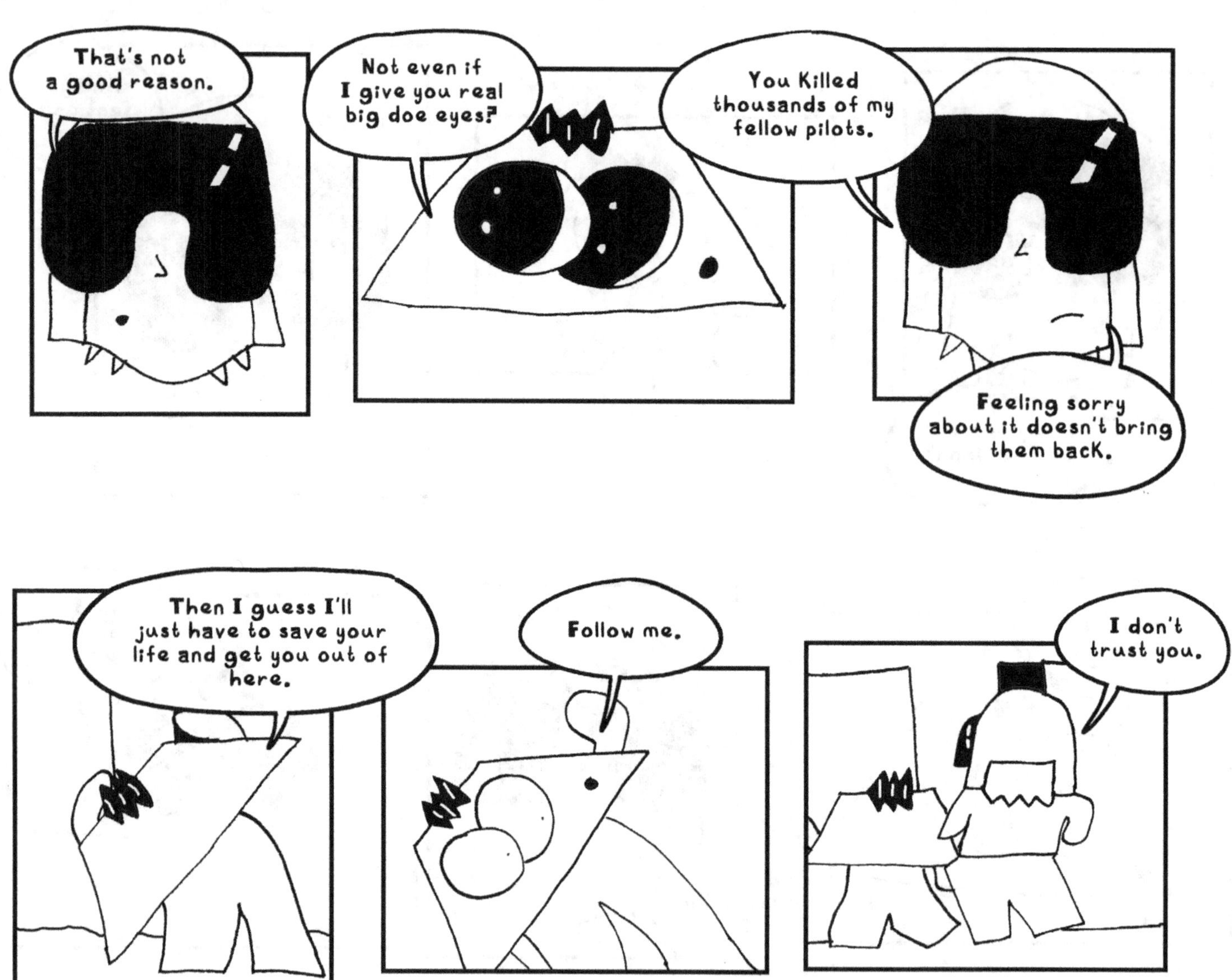

That's not a good reason.
Not even if I give you real big doe eyes?
You Killed thousands of my fellow pilots.
Feeling sorry about it doesn't bring them back.
Then I guess I'll just have to save your life and get you out of here.
Follow me.
I don't trust you.

Probably
a good instinct.

Bring in
the prisoner.

Yes, sir.

This is gonna
fix everything.

Mr. General, sir?
So, you're the alien who started this all.
I'm not—
Don't interrupt me, boy!
Sorry, sir.
Not yet.
But you will be.

So, we failed, huh?
Real bad.

This is all my fault.

I just wanted to save the world.
Well, that's a pretty big order, especially for a twelve-year-old Kid.
Harry Potter did it.
Harry Potter is better than you.
He's also fictional.

Don't you thinK I Know that?!
But, dude, at least you tried something, and that's not nothing.
Even if you failed real bad.
I guess that's true.

I need to talk to my people.
You don't get needs, boy.
I get needs.
You get a bowl of hush.
I mean, okay, but I can end the war, I think.
End the war?
You expect me to believe that you want to end the war?
Nah, you're up to something.
Something nefarious.

Where is Rectavius?!
What's a Rectavius?
Don't play dumb with me.
I'm not playing!
So you really are this dumb?
Are all humans this dumb?
We're not dumb, ma'am.
Knowledge is not the same as intelligence.
I know that!

Now, I'm going to give your people one last chance to end this before I 'splode your whole planet.

BZZT
CLICK

Surrender!

If you don't, I will totally do bad things to your planet.

Real bad.

Okay.

We surrender.
Wait!
Look what we have!
An alien!
My name is Rectavius Triangulo.
Move over!
I don't know what game you're playing. but look at this.
Reck!

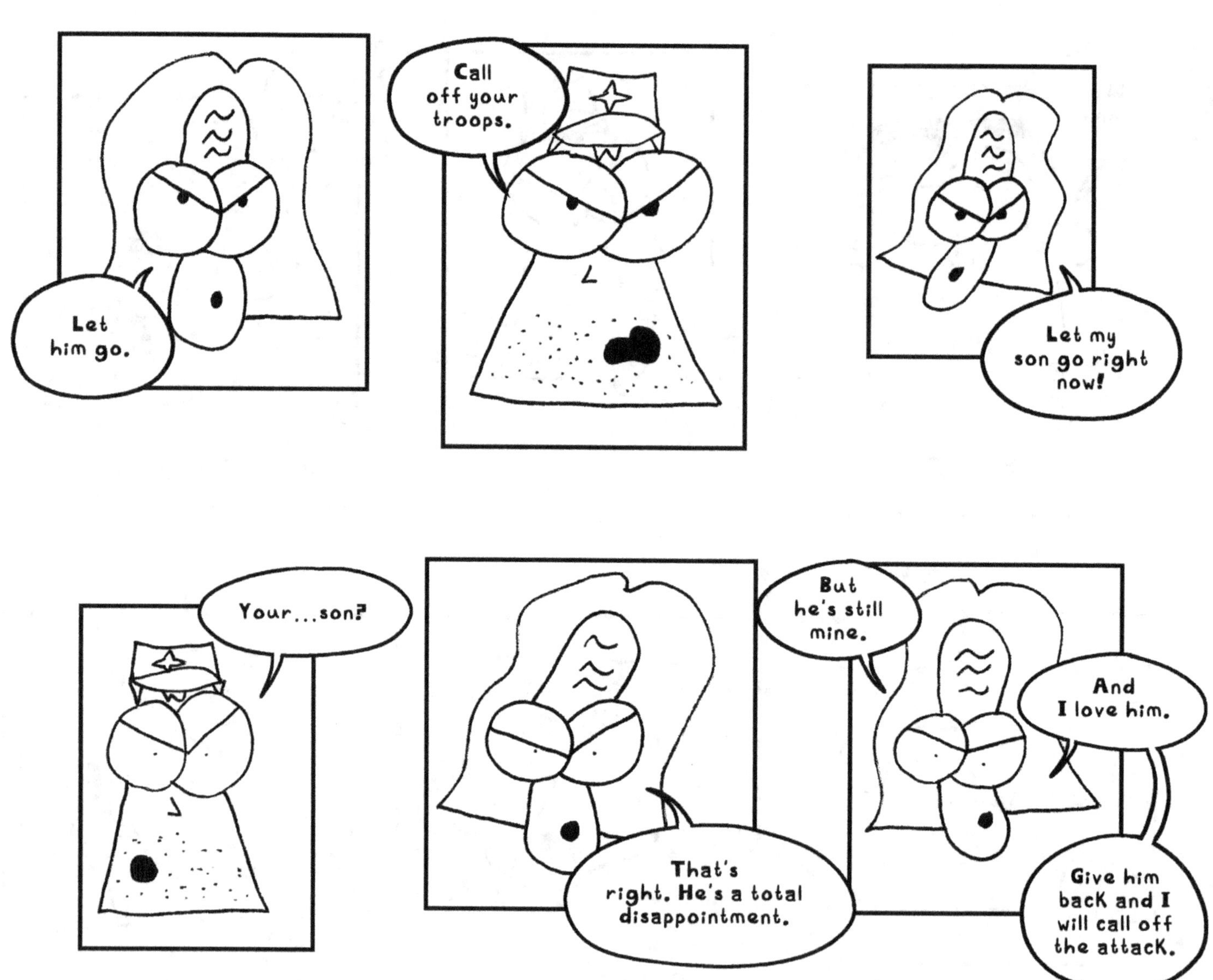

Let
him go.
Call
off your
troops.
Let my
son go right
now!
Your...son?
But
he's still
mine.
And
I love him.
That's
right. He's a total
disappointment.
Give him
back and I
will call off
the attack.

So if we just give this weird thing back, then you'll stop the invasion?
You should do that. She's very unreasonable usually.
Yeah, I am on board with this plan.
As long as nobody calls me a wimp.
I promise to never do that.
And now, on this historic day, a peace accord has been signed by our two great planets.

And I would like to thank the Venusian leader for not killing us all.

Thank you.
CLAP
CLAP

Would you come say a few words?

Thank you, Earth.
Your planet smells like a foot.
And you are all psychotic apes.
It would be so easy to destroy your whole planet.

Please don't.

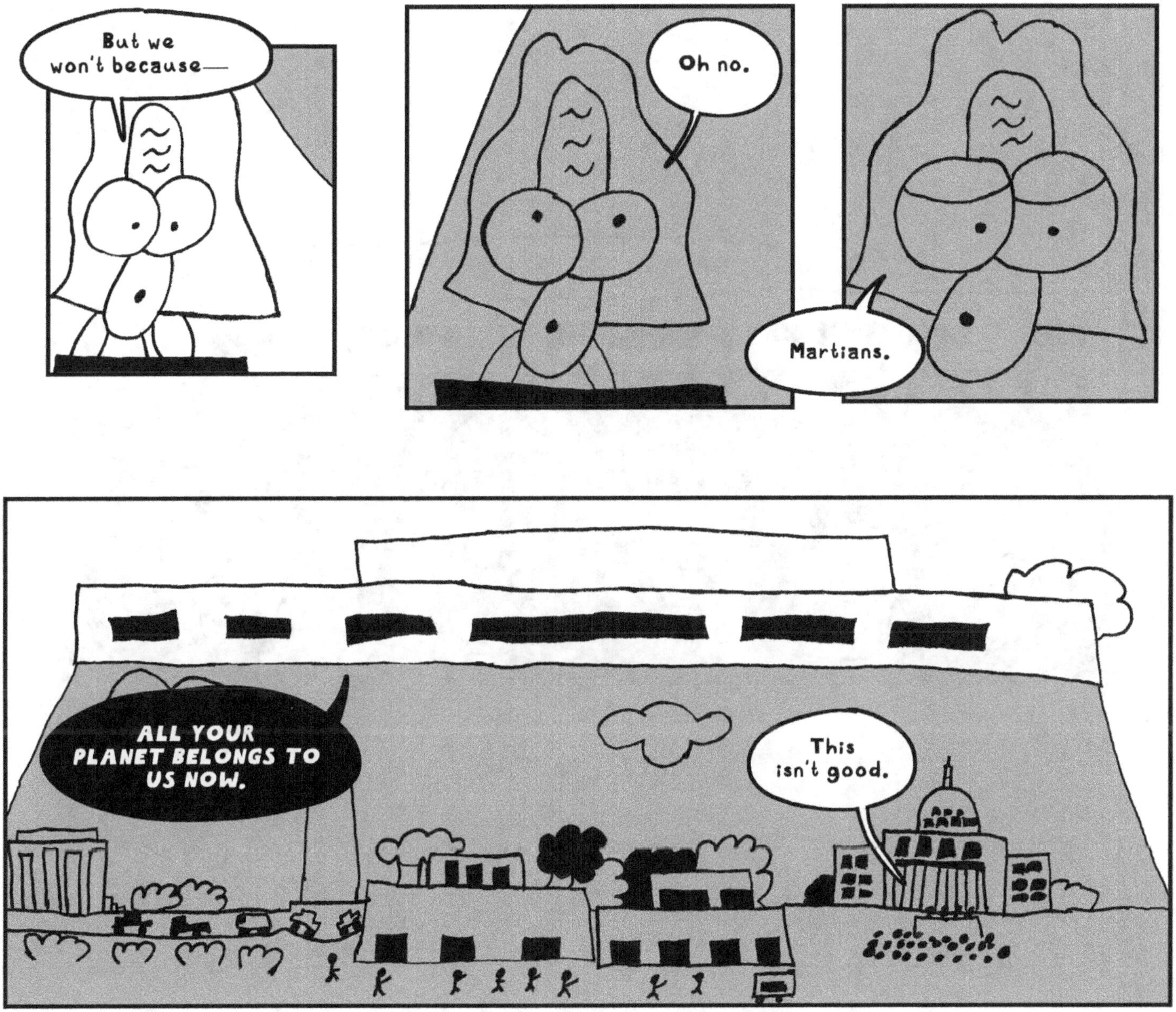

ALL YOUR PLANET BELONGS TO US NOW.

This isn't good.

MERCIFULLY, THE END.

You just read this booK.

It happened.

I hope you liKed it.

But whether you liKed it or not, you read it. For the rest
of your life, you will have never not read this booK. Sit with
that for a minute. How does it feel?

Hope it feels good.

For what it's worth, for the rest of my life, I will have never
not released this booK. We are bonded by that truth. I drew
this booK **FIVE** years ago, and I have been absolutely **PETRIFIED**
of sharing it with you.

Why now? I don't Know, honestly. It just felt right in this absurd time to
release an absurd booK.

I'm still petrified, because it is **SOOO** different from everything
else I've ever done in my career, with the exception of GherKin Boy,
which I also drew.

I find it completely absurd that I drew two comic booKs, and that
people have enjoyed them as much as they have.

Or maybe I'm getting ahead of myself to assume you liKed this booK.
I hope you did though, and if you did then you are my Kind of human.

My Process:

Step one:

It started when I found some sketch pads that were the same size as a comic strip. For Gherkin Boy, I used a nine by twelve pad, but this was different. I have a hard time using just part of a pad. I need the perfect size for the project.

I start out in ink, specifically a fine point sharpie. I know that sounds bonkers because sharpies give almost no control, but that's my proecess, for better or worse. In the middle of the book, I stopped doing any shading at all, but in the beginning, I did it like this.

My Process:

Step two:

After the page is scanned in, I select all the line worK and, on a new layer, redraw and digitally inK all the sharpie worK. Once that's done, I finish all the fine details, liKe the wires on panel three. I'm aware there's not much fine detail, but for me that's pretty fine.

Once the digital inKs are laid, then I finish with the panel borders. I try to Keep the original pages as simple as possible, because almost all of the worK is done in Photoshop.

My Process:

Step three:

The pages were sent to **Cammry** for lettering, and I have to say that I love how they turned out. I thought that my work was quite crude and ugly, but somehow **Cammry** made it look like my style was intentional and not just the peak of my ability.

The lettering came from having a little bit of extra money from the **Ichabod Jones: Monster Hunter** volume two campaign, and the fact I was working with **Cammry** on another project. I'm so thrilled with how it turned out.

I know lots of people have a much longer process, but mine is pretty quick, as you can probably tell by the end style.

Sometimes, you have to cut a panel or page for pacing or story flow.

Here are some of my favorite panels that were left on the cutting room floor.

Trap was bored one day, so he decided to blow up the Moon. This ended up being a bad idea, as it turned out that humans had strong feels about the silly, little thing.

9 781942 350606